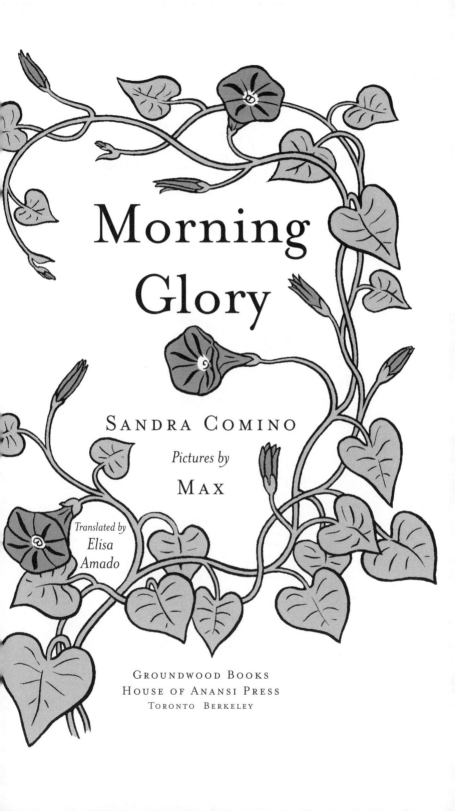

Morning Glory

SANDRA COMINO

Pictures by

MAX

Translated by
Elisa
Amado

GROUNDWOOD BOOKS
HOUSE OF ANANSI PRESS
TORONTO BERKELEY

Groundwood Books / House of Anansi Press
110 Spadina Avenue, Suite 801, Toronto, ON, M5V 2K4

Distributed in the USA by Publishers Group West
1700 Fourth Street, Berkeley, CA 94710

We acknowledge for their financial support of our publishing
program the Canada Council for the Arts, the Government of
Canada through the Book Publishing Industry Development
Program (BPIDP) and the Ontario Arts Council.

ONTARIO ARTS COUNCIL
CONSEIL DES ARTS DE L'ONTARIO

Library and Archives Canada Cataloging in Publication
Comino, Sandra
Morning glory / by Sandra Comino; translated by Elisa Amado;
illustrated by Max.
Translation of: La enamorada del muro.
ISBN-13: 978-0-88899-642-8 (bound) –
ISBN-10: 0-88899-642-X (bound) –
ISBN-13: 978-0-88899-643-5 (pbk.) –
ISBN-10: 0-88899-643-8 (pbk.)
I. Amado, Elisa II. Max III. Title.
PZ7.C748Mo 2006   j863'.7   C2006-901932-0

Printed and bound in Canada
Design by Michael Solomon

To Diana, who tells this story just right.

— S.C.

To Julia

— Max

It *all began one morning* when Ivan saw what he saw on the morning glory vine that grew up the back wall. That was when the whole schmozzle began. That's how what happened, happened.

Until that moment, every morning in the life of Ivan and his mother, Eulogia, seemed to go by pretty much the same, day in and day out. After breakfast Eulogia always went out shopping while Ivan sat at the kitchen table to do his homework before school.

Ivan would sit by the window, surrounded by
his books. But instead of looking at his work,
his eyes always seemed to shift to the courtyard
outside. They would wander over to the wall
and stare at the morning glory vine whose
tendrils and leaves climbed lushly up a trellis
and even crept over onto the neighbor's walls.
Most fascinating were the beautiful bright
blue flowers that his eyes feasted on for
minutes, maybe even hours at a time.

The only thing that could bring Ivan out of his dreamy contemplation of the morning glory was his mother's return. She'd throw open the door and bang her parcels down on the kitchen counter.

"Have you gone to the moon, son?" she'd ask loudly.

"No, Mum," he'd reply, hoping not to catch a scolding. "I'm in math land."

It was always the same, day in and day out, until the day when Ivan saw what he saw and what happened, happened.

One April morning, just at the moment when his mother opened the door on her way back from shopping, just before she banged her bags down on the kitchen counter and asked if he had gone to the moon, Ivan saw a gigantic female rat crawling up the wall and over onto the morning glory.

This was the moment when that morning stopped being just like every other morning that came around, day in and day out. He felt a scream rush out of his mouth and he hurled it straight at the rat. His mother, startled out of her wits by this incredibly loud noise, dropped the bags on the floor. Following his scream with her eyes, she saw the rat sitting on the morning glory and let out an equally piercing scream of her own. The screams arrived at the morning glory with such force that the rat lost her balance and fell to the ground with a crash.

The morning glory trembled.

Mother and son, their faces as white as paper from the panic they were feeling, milled around, forward and backward, tripping over each other.

Finally they felt brave enough to run down and inspect the rat. She seemed to be dead. Then they both gathered up their strength and screamed once again, so loudly that they could be heard on the street. The baker, the greengrocer, the barber and the postman all burst into the courtyard without even knocking.

The neighbor across the street thought there must be a fire and called the firefighters.

The baker's wife thought it must be a robber and called the police.

The butcher, for fear that there had been an
accident, called the ambulance and the
store-keeper called the radio and TV stations.
They were the first to arrive.

Ivan decided to go upstairs and watch the
news on TV.

Everyone was crowded in the street outside
the house waiting to see what had happened.

Ivan's father, Feliciano, closed up his
woodworking shop at exactly twelve o'clock, as
he always did, and went home for lunch.
When he saw the crowds outside his house,
his heart began to beat fast, his stomach
began to burn, and his legs felt oddly weak
and feeble.

"She's dead, all right," said a fireman who was just leaving.

And Feliciano thought that *she* must be his wife.

"Don't cry, man, the city is full of creatures like this," said the fireman, scratching his head. "Crying over a rat," he murmured to himself. But Feliciano couldn't hear him because the siren on the fire engine was still wailing.

The police pushed their way through the crowd. The ambulance pulled up and double-parked. The reporters from the radio and TV stations stood outside reporting that someone or something had died near the morning glory, but they weren't sure exactly who or what.

The policeman, who was a stickler for procedure, told Eulogia to remove the rat's corpse. But first she'd have to get permission from the Humane Society.

Off she went, dutifully, and everyone stood around waiting for her to come back. But the crowds were so great that she didn't see her husband who was huddled against the wall crying.

On Channel 33 the hairdresser was telling a reporter, "They say she fell off the trellis. But the body can't be moved until the coroner comes. Neither the police nor the firefighters nor the ambulance can do anything without the coroner," she said importantly.

On the street Feliciano overheard and moaned, "I begged her not to prune that morning glory."

Upstairs Ivan sighed, turned off the TV and decided to go back to bed. He slammed his bedroom door shut to keep out the noise.

It took Eulogia a few minutes to find the Humane Society. She was feeling quite distraught as she put her head around the door. There was no one at the front desk. So she yelled out and took her shoe off to pound the desk with her heel.

A red-haired woman wearing bright red lipstick that matched her hair looked out from an office and said, "Leave a note saying what you want and come back in forty-five days for an answer."

"I can't wait!" shouted Eulogia.

"Then go up to the Emergency Office on the second floor," said the red-headed woman as she slammed the door.

At home the crowds were becoming restless.
More and more people arrived and there was
murmuring and shoving. One of the
reporters was shouting into her microphone,
"This is an exclusive. The firemen have
covered the body because they don't want us
to see what has happened."

Feliciano sobbed. He didn't want to hear any
more.

Eulogia had climbed up to the second floor of the Humane Society. A woman at the desk said, "It's lunchtime, miss. Take a number if you like and wait."

"But you're the only one here," said Eulogia.

"You still have to wait," the woman replied.

"But she's dead!" said Eulogia. "The policeman told me I couldn't take the body away until an inspector comes. My son saw her fall."

"Oh well, then," said the woman. "If it's a death, go up to the fifth floor."

When Eulogia staggered up to the fifth floor she found a sign that said, "This floor is closed because of a civil service strike. Emergencies will be attended to at Emergency Services, 225 Quick Street downtown."

Feliciano had made his way into the
apartment where he sat crying in the
bathroom.

"Stop crying," said a curious neighbor
who had just walked in. "Don't be such a
weakling. It's not worth it."

By then Eulogia had arrived at Emergency Services and was talking to a young man at the front desk. He was sitting reading the paper.

"It's time to take the body away!" she demanded.

"For that you've got to go to the Fatal Accidents Directorate, Madam," he said. "It's at 500 Quick Street."

The neighbors at Eulogia's house had made
coffee for everyone. Feliciano had to make his
own chamomile tea. A voice could be heard
yelling at the reporters.

"You can't come in. We'll give you access
when it's time."

"Line up, please," a woman said to Eulogia when she arrived at last at the Fatal Accidents Directorate.

"What line? I don't see anyone," she replied.

"Line up anyway," said the woman and she went back to painting her nails.

Eulogia was willing to try anything. She stepped back while the woman finished her nails. She watched her as she screwed the lid of the nail polish on tight, without smudging the polish, and put the bottle back in her purse. Then, blowing on her nails, the woman said, "Next in line, please."

Eulogia told her the whole story and only exaggerated a little.

Feliciano had just finished his tea when a policeman stormed in. "Are you the owner of the house? You have to come and see the body. What, are you scared? You aren't worth much, are you?"

Feliciano suddenly remembered Ivan and wondered what had become of his son. This only made him feel worse.

Eulogia had finally managed to get the woman with the freshly painted nails to send her directly to the office of the inspector himself, but only because it was such an emergency. He was so very kind to her that she wondered if she'd fallen asleep and was dreaming.

With the help of the neighbors, policemen had dragged Feliciano out to the garden and were confronting him with the cloth-covered cadaver.

"Nooooo! I can't bear to see her. I want to remember her the way she was," he wailed.

The policeman leaned over to uncover the body, but stopped when he realized that Feliciano was walking dejectedly back into the house.

Just then, Eulogia came in and saw her husband.

"Can you believe what's been happening, old man?" she said. "I'm dead!"

"Oh my God," said Feliciano. "I'm seeing her and she's telling me she's dead. And where's Ivan, anyway?" And he burst into tears once again.

Everyone was so busy watching this pathetic scene, nobody noticed that the cloth was moving. Slowly the cadaver made its way between people's legs.

Looking at the empty spot on the ground, the inspector asked the hairdresser, "Well, where's the body, then?"

"Look, Mister Inspector, you'd best ask the owner of the house. I don't want anyone saying that we neighbors are busybodies." Then she stopped. "Hey," she shouted. "She's getting away!"

As the rat picked up speed, Feliciano ran after her. Eulogia ran after him and the inspector followed close behind. The policemen started running after the inspector who was running after Eulogia who was running after Feliciano. The ambulance driver ran after the policemen who ran after the inspector who was running after Eulogia who was trying to grab Feliciano. Behind them streamed the baker, the greengrocer, and the radio and TV reporters.

The shouts finally woke Ivan up. He came sleepily to the door. But when he saw what was happening, he ran as fast as he could after the baker, the greengrocer, and the radio and TV reporters who were running after the ambulance driver who ran after the policemen who ran after the inspector who was running after Eulogia who had managed to grab Feliciano.

Meanwhile, back at home, the wind was dancing with the beautiful flowers of the morning glory that was finally all alone on the wall in the empty courtyard.